# TURKANA BOY

# TURKANA BOY

## Jean-François Beauchemin

Translated by Jessica Moore

Talonbooks

Copyright © 2004 French language edition: Éditions Québec Amérique
Translation copyright © 2012 Jessica Moore

Talonbooks
P.O. Box 2076
Vancouver, British Columbia, Canada V6B 3S3
www.talonbooks.com

Typeset in Arno and printed and bound in Canada.
Printed on 50% post-consumer recycled paper.
Typeset by Typesmith.

First printing: 2012

The publisher gratefully acknowledges the financial support of the Canada
Council for the Arts, the Government of Canada through the Canada
Book Fund, and the Province of British Columbia through the British
Columbia Arts Council and the Book Publishing Tax Credit for our pub-
lishing activities.

*Turkana Boy* by Jean-François Beauchemin was first published in French in
2004 by Éditions Québec Amérique. We acknowledge the financial support
of the Government of Canada through the National Translation Program for
Book Publishing, for our publishing activities.

Beauchemin, Jean-François, 1960–
[Turkana Boy. English]
    Turkana Boy / Jean-François Beauchemin ; translated by Jessica Moore.

Translation of: Turkana Boy.
ISBN 978-0-88922-690-6

    I. Moore, Jessica, 1978– II. Title. III. Title: Turkana Boy. English.

PS8553.E17176T8713 2012        C843'.54        C2011-908718-9

In the memory of my Father

*– Sainte-Anne-des-Lacs,*
*Quebec, Winter 2004*

When I walked outside the building on Central Park West, I looked across at the trees that had burst into full leaf and had a sensation of ineffable strangeness. Being alive is inexplicable, I thought. Consciousness itself is inexplicable. There is nothing ordinary in the world.

— SIRI HUSTVEDT
*What I Loved*

# 1

## The Escaped Island

He took notes. All his life, Monsieur Bartolomé had done nothing but take notes. He gave titles to downpours, produced chapters in which ordinary things occurred; in his stories, he always wrote birds onto the first page. Sometimes he made books of these stories, in which people said they recognized the glimmerings of childhood. But this was too easy to say – he was not interested in childhood – it had taken years for his own to hush a little, and anyway he preferred the bitter beauty of things. In his books, there was always this misunderstanding: the children he described were not children, but adults – who still had a quality about them that made you think of childhood but was in fact something completely different, something that had taken Monsieur Bartolomé a long time to name.

One day, reading over a few passages here and there, he realized that all the people in his stories had this in common: they were men and women waiting for some advent, solitary souls who could not live without others, dreamers shattered by reality, lovers who did not know what to do with their intelligence, free beings imprisoned inside themselves. Then he understood why people saw so much of childhood in his writing – without realizing it, he had created a little society of maladjusted people who did not yet understand the world in which they lived. He had depicted beings who, in their own fashion, took notes for later, gave titles to the rains so that they might recognize them if they ever came back. But each rain was different and none fell on the world more than once – this was doubtlessly why Monsieur Bartolomé was so fascinated by them. This was also why he preferred birds. Because birds did come back, and always from afar, as though preceding humans in their ceaseless march towards the future.

He had a young son. He was a calm child, full of silences, who played his games in the shadow of an immense elm planted in the yard, miraculous escapee of the big city's tentacles. The years in those times passed like the shadow of the elm over the young boy's back: light, long, cool, harbouring the projects of birds.

The child had always said: "This tree is my brother." Then, one day, the elm had to be taken down – disease had invaded the leaves, the bark, and every other part of it. Workers came with chainsaws. With his nose crushed against the window, Monsieur Bartolomé's son watched the branches give way one by one. Then the workers left. The child dragged his feet in the debris for an hour. For him, childhood ended there. Maybe that was his first sadness, who knows? But something else had fallen with the branches and lay beneath his feet, in the dust of the tree that was now and would always be inconceivably smaller than him. The yard was inundated with light. It was the only time he shouted insults at the sun.

3

Monsieur Bartolomé was hardly an expert on things of the sky.
Human prayer, the leafy tops of tall trees, certain kinds of music
as well: everything that had its place up there remained foreign
to him, far away. Monsieur Bartolomé's universe was made up
of streets, houses, cars, chairs, notebooks, and loose change. He
had been thrown in chains in a hold called earth. So how to
speak of this call for aerial things that resounded within him,
of this space that unfurled itself, vast as a firmament? Because
nothing, truly, is more anchored, more terrestrial than the body.
How to name this light thing tied to the ballast of the limbs, the
organs, the bones, and the blood? The soul? Was the soul, then,
a sky tangled in every person?

Besides, the sky did not usually mix with the earth. But it happened sometimes that – the dawn's colours stretching out farther than usual – the earth rushed towards the sky and blended with it. This mixture painted an image of the hours to come, announcing a rare concordance of things terrestrial and celestial. At those times, highways overtook the sun. A plane passed, dreaming of roads. Houses became animated, baptized by a rain. Then it was twilight: in the angled rooftops of the bell towers, windowpanes fell asleep. Leaning against his window, Monsieur Bartolomé bathed his face in the last light. The park was watched over by stars, those islands.

His hands were like soldiers coming home from conquered countries: recognizable only by the wounds written on their sides. His hands were caverns, hoarding their shadows and leaving people to their late-evening lanterns. His hands were valleys hemmed in by dreams: one could hear within them the far-off echo of gestures made long before. His hands were cities with metered lights, with market stalls of schedules, with people at their windows.

Water threaded between his fingers until it was no more than a glove of dreams: soon his hand closed again over this fleeting stuff that, already, could only be proven by the fever it had eased. But bread was different, and always left something behind: a white veil lay over his skin, torn here and there by dips and swells, the undulations of the palm. The ocean, boats, had passed this way. Monsieur Bartolomé liked that his hand was the landscape of these things. He liked that bread and water passed over it, leaving a trace as tangible as a snowfall of flour, as barely visible as a sated thirst.

In his youth he had, just like his son, chosen silence. Still so young, he had not been able to make it an ally – it was too soon. But already he could feel that a day would come when his brow, his hands, and his steps would grow quieter. Then something would begin – the height of youth would be over. As he waited, he learned to recognize the first signs of the inward turning to come. Because he was still little, he did not attribute much importance to these things: the wind climbing the walls and blowing wickedly, the hours that passed over things with the sounds of ends to come. Already it seemed to him that when boats left port they left with low voices.

And now that was done, now that childhood, adolescence, and the first years of adulthood had passed, something was coming – he could feel it.

7

He remembered evenings like the hulls of ships. He descended to them like trees to their roots and pressed his ear to their iron, gathering, as though he were filling a basket. There he found refuge from the planet's noise. There he saw riverbanks teeming with newborn animals impatient to run. At the window of his house was no bird seeking the wind, only the moon clinging to its dark side. In the hours when the window washer rested, Monsieur Bartolomé went out and wrote upon the walls of the city two questions he would carry with him all his life, beneath his jacket: *Will I have been a good inhabitant of the earth? Whose student will I have been?*

12

At night, he got up to watch the rain, its narrow dance. The sky then was no longer the same – all the streaks of light had left, and nothing was left overhead but the slow bellies of whales trailing their spray. This fell to earth like a night, and Monsieur Bartolomé thought to himself: *The rain is always a night upon the night.* He had always loved this somewhat fearful marriage of rain and the night, this union of elusive things that descend upon us in the deepest hours. He would stay at the window for a long time, upright like the drops; he did not know how to explain this miracle of water that rises above everything and falls again like the tears of heavy animals.

9

Things, objects, inspired in him the highest respect. The hammered stone, outlined in fire, that in ancient times gave rise to human beings and their skyward omens. Tables whose cloths conjured dreams and feasts. Ink that cracked over words. Even this paper that led them, folded, to his few readers. This chair where he sat for a moment's rest. All the spades driven into the ground, delving into the rich earth of vegetable gardens. The coat embracing the body. The window where thoughts were composed in the lovely order of half-closed lashes. The lamp, the lamp that he carried in his fist, its light always leaning towards evening.

Every day was like a new land. Monsieur Bartolomé approached each one like a sailor dropping anchor on the fringes of an island, feeling like he was taking possession of a world both open and closed, free and captive: surrounded by a sea. More than anything, the solitude of that world seduced him. With the exception of his son, whose presence he always tried to prolong, he wanted others to leave him to his retreat so that he could continue to build inside himself, according to his own plans, the dwelling place he had begun one day, he could not remember when. This had nothing to do with misanthropy. He simply needed the kind of insular withdrawal that he could only find within himself. Most often, he went there to find peaceful coves, calm and affable crabs, shipwrecked yet nourishing hulls.

He had read, in his early years, the extraordinary adventure of *Robinson Crusoe*. One thing had struck his imagination more than any other detail of the text: that this time away from almost all other civilization could have been a source of such unhappiness for the famous castaway. Because Robinson, wishing relentlessly for an end to his confinement on the island, did not rest until the crew of a vessel, appearing finally on the shore, delivered him from the hell where fate had tossed him some twenty-eight years earlier. Why such despair, Monsieur Bartolomé had wondered when he was eleven, turning the pages of this fabulous book for the first time, this cornerstone of his human career. He never saw in that character, recluse among recluses, anything but the most fortunate of men. A free man, or almost free: surrounded by himself, only himself.

Some evenings, the wind roped the buildings together and hauled the city away like a boat on the waves. Except that it was a strange voyage, full of movement, yes, but movement quickly aborted: the city resisted, anchored by its burrows of light.

The child had been put to bed and had fallen asleep, entrusted to the care of a good and generous neighbour, and now Monsieur Bartolomé left the house for an adventure in the streets. He fell in with the crowd. Not that he was seeking a sense of belonging – that would have been a sign linking him to humanity, and he felt so little relation to it. His quest was elsewhere – halfway, it seemed to him, between earth and sky. He slipped the reins through the harness of stars.

Bit by bit, the city forged halos of light – the first bright bands gathered on landings. Crowds pressed together on street corners: there stood the portrait of a century. Then it was the hour when the high towers lit up. At their feet, the boulevards were spliced by steamers, sparkling and upright. Taxis carried young people unballasted of their deaths to board them, docking at forests of buildings. Tides stopped at red lights. He walked in this night of noises and unreality, in this sea of faces, bodies, laughter, light, and words. His face was reflected in the windows. The hours passed, the night did its job.

In the end, the rising dawn recruited Monsieur Bartolomé. Ads dozed in the windowpanes. A street lamp coughed and went out. Once, he had read on the front page of the newspaper: *God Is Dead*. But what did that matter to him – God and his biting wing, his deaf silence? Time resounded in the years like water in parched jars. Monsieur Bartolomé was young.

Poets, among others, made the abdomen a symbol of fertility – of all beginnings. It seemed to Monsieur Bartolomé that, on the contrary, death had made its nest in his belly. His end was resting inside him. Was not the abdomen the first place that nourishment went, the receptacle on which all life depended; and upon leaving the world, did the belly not determine what would come next – did it not even program the end? There, in the hollows and folds, a sun was in slow decline; one day, burned to ashes, it would breathe white into his hair, and little by little, the sureness of his step would grow cold. Something lay there – a reminder of the brevity of days: yesterday, Monsieur Bartolomé had been a child; now here he was, an adult. From the very beginning, death had been placed in the centre of his body like an important message written in the middle of the page. So for him, the poets were mistaken: the abdomen was not the synonym of beginnings. In fact, he felt that it was exactly the opposite. "I came into existence beginning with death," he often said to himself. All the time that would pass from his birth onward would be charged with this singular reality. Each day, he thought to himself: *In the end, I will be born.*

Laws were written on walls, on packages, and on street signs;
in the courts, at customs, and on street corners. These laws
did not mean much to him; he went to places where more
interesting things awaited: he sat on terraces and watched
the slow-growing edifice of cars, stretching out alongside the
crowds. He liked these crowds, too, loaded with souls and haste,
swelling with eccentric pregnancies. On high-perched roofs,
cranes approached the flocks contained within the clouds.
Their metal ate the height in mouthfuls, bit at the real like the
dawn at new fruit. A rain descended, threw its fibre on the
world. Suddenly, a flight of coal: darkness. The skyscrapers fell
into the lake to the right of Ursa Major. These were the days of
Monsieur Bartolomé on earth, his gaze turned towards the light.

14

And then one day, something terrible happened.

Monsieur Bartolomé lost his son. On that day, the child, now twelve years old, disappeared without a trace. No one saw him again. Did he run away? Was he kidnapped? Was there an accident? No one knew.

An investigation ensued, of course; leads were followed, all of which proved false. The neighbour who sometimes looked after him was questioned. Nothing showed in her apart from that sort of distress invading the features that is, one might say, the face's translation of great sorrows rising from the depths of being. In short, whatever the cause, the child's disappearance remained a mystery.

On that day, for Monsieur Bartolomé, youth died. On that day, the house died. In the street, the neighbours lowered their eyes as they passed, sensing that just there, so close, Monsieur Bartolomé was crying all around the little bed. On that day, the city died, and on that day, half of everything died. Monsieur Bartolomé was like a book unmasted. He had just lost the greatest part of himself, everything that, for twelve years, had made him a human being among human beings.

In the months that followed, he left the city many times and went walking in the forests where the bustle of intersections and grand avenues could not reach him, because Monsieur Bartolomé often thought of the tree the child had so loved, and even more often, of the sky that stood over it through the years. Monsieur Bartolomé would not have known how to say why, but it was clear that he needed this sky now, resting on the tops of trees like a benevolent hand blessing them.

He wandered like this for long hours through the fields, on the pathways, and in the shade of the woods. Dust from the paths inscribed his age upon his ankles. Often, nothing stirred – even the leaves hung from branches as though from coat hangers. In the groves, animals dreamed their grammar of shadows. Then – all of a sudden – clouds of birds would pass, as though they had just been reminded of their duty. He thought of the Sunday when the child had been seen for the last time. Suddenly things had been more serious than usual. It would always be so, from that moment onward.

When he got home, he struggled to find sleep, and when, broken by fatigue, he finally sank into it, he often dreamed a strange dream. His dog, who had died years earlier, was running towards him. At the same moment that he felt the big yellow paws of the animal in his hands, Monsieur Bartolomé raised his eyes and saw his son smiling on the doorstep of the house. The child was holding a large ball in his arms and one might have said that the ball was his whole life, held, held back like that between his two small arms, too short still.

Upon waking, this thought stayed for a long time in Monsieur Bartolomé's grieving mind: *We say certain things are unspeakable, but I don't believe it. Are not languages our own invention? So they are both made of the same stuff. One day I will know the words to describe the extraordinary joy, mixed with sorrow, that I felt again last night.*

He would go to collect himself in the small room that had become useless. The child did not see his father's lips gloved with the old song, nor the spear in his pierced heart; he did not hear this man's voice speaking his name. Because his name was lost in the twists and turns of painful memories. And his name was a hull stranded on a sandbank of shadows.

He would open the window and listen to the world rustling. He could see storms far away, bringing, as they came closer, the murmur of tired birds who had returned to say: "We see nothing now but imprisoned suns. Surrender marks the eyes of people darkly, and they say that tomorrow, rains will stumble upon the stones."

He touched his forehead: a fever made it hot. He wished that one of those exhausted birds, rain folded under its wing, would come and sit there.

Higher up, there surely breathed skies that escaped the senses. He intuited their existence, as one might divine the roots of trees beneath the soil, creeping towards the underbellies of pathways. He wanted to know these skies. He hoped that corridors would be lifted upwards. He accompanied crowds in their encasement of buses, then climbed with them the long vine of escalators. In attics, he received news of planes and sparrows. A chair was held for him on the rooftops. He wrote the itinerary of smoke in notebooks, sent telegraphs to blackbirds, assigned missions to air balloons. Then he went home. He would have liked to have a dog waiting for him, running to meet him, wagging his tail. The words enchained in the animal's body would have lived a brief life on its muzzle – and would have made, like an unexpected dance in the hollow of his hand, a sky.

It was simply that the world was too small. Monsieur Bartolomé had to lift his gaze above the limits of his enclosure. He loved space, and the inhabitants of its vast prairie: meteors, planets, stars, and suns, but also airplanes, missiles, and rockets. Because they made it possible to wander out there, and then return, bringing back fragments of science, a light that translated worlds. He was captivated by the incredible vessels catapulted up there, inhabited by people whose hands were gloved with air, occupied with their fabulous expeditions. At times, a mechanical breakdown forced them to take light steps outside. Then they were suspended from nothingness as from dreams. One false move, one meteoric distraction, and a tool would slip from a glove, condemned to spin towards the full infinity of orbits, to slide forever between the assemblies of stars. Ah! The laughable enlargement of our human domain! And yet, there were few dawns when Monsieur Bartolomé did not dream of those pliers, that fugitive key, moving towards the next continents.

He copied out in his notebook the words that always troubled him, and that he had read many times in *Memoirs of Hadrian* by Marguerite Yourcenar: "This morning it occurred to me for the first time that my body, my faithful companion and friend, truer and better known to me than my own soul, may be after all only a sly beast who will end by devouring his master."

As though in echo to these words, sudden memories of the child came flashing back, striking against him like a vehement fever. Lightning pierced his flesh, and a raging sea full of shards of broken glass flung itself relentlessly against his sides. Pain itself was incarnate in his voice; it made dark circles under his eyes, a reminder of the skeleton buried long ago beneath his skin. His hour approached.

Peace, after such torment, took on extraordinary significance. Monsieur Bartolomé welcomed it with the thirst of one who has been brought back from the dead. This peace took the form of silence – a particular, rare silence. A silence of the organs, inert: permeated with death. It was at these times above all that he learned that death accompanied him even in the hours when he was most alive – that it was hidden away inside him. Inert. He knew it was waiting, waiting for him, silent, peaceful, and that it was not ugly.

But there was a light in the middle of the body's shadows: the skeleton, that white vessel spangled with foam, immobile on a sea enclosed by the skin and on which the organs, muscles, mother-of-pearl, and tissue formed strange pieces of flotsam. The skeleton, though anchored, still covered its share of distances. Its movement was not calculated leaning over maps, with instruments of copper worn down by the salt on fingertips. It was a progress of hands lined with confessions, of seedlings threaded through the eye of the earth, an extension of fields: the mark of time upon each of us from the moment of our birth.

He entered cemeteries gladly. When he pushed open their iron gates, a peace came over him almost as great as the feeling of his body revived from a fever. Clearly he found, in these narrow rows carved out by contemplation, comfort of a kind: how complete it was, the silence of the departed! Monsieur Bartolomé moved across the lawns and the only shadow falling upon him was that of the oaks. He read loving words engraved on the tombstones by those who had survived. This thought came to him: *Nowhere else are love and death so intimately linked than here.* Maybe eternity had something to do with it. He observed the trees. He knew their roots attended to the dead – they were engaged in the mysterious and contradictory work of chaining to the earth bodies that were now so completely free.

It was not during his visits to the cemetery that the strongest images of his son came back to him. Because he still continued to hope that he would see him again, alive, and not once had he imagined him dead. No, it was the sea, seen on television or in ads postered around town, for example, that most often made recollections of the child rise up from the folds of his memory.

One day while he was lingering in front of one of these posters, he said to himself: "I was the father of an island." Because, in his mind, the child had possessed every characteristic of an island. He was alone, surrounded, upright, inhabited by lives and dangers that belonged only to him. There were times when the tides had undone him, just as they do with beaches: disappointments, alarms, or various drowned things would surface unexpectedly. But the tides also brought bottles whose bodies had unwound secret beckonings. Monsieur Bartolomé had dreamed of knowing the secrets enclosed within his son. His whole life as a father had been dedicated to this quest. Up until the day the workers had come to take down the elm, the child, in keeping with his secrets there, perhaps, had scattered behind him little bits of childhood, small crumbs. For a long time Monsieur Bartolomé had gathered them, prolonging his own dawns with this bread. He had gathered them in the incongruous hope that he could give them back to his son one day (or at least give him back some of that aerial lightness of the trees) once the more difficult days of adulthood had come.

In front of the poster, Monsieur Bartolomé thought to himself: *I was the father of an island.* Then, turning his eyes away: *Here I am now, the father of a boat.*

What is a boat? An island that has escaped.

23

God was of little importance to him. Still, Monsieur Bartolomé stopped at almost all the churches he passed along the way. The bells, like airplanes, meteors, edifices, and tall trees, exercised the same mute pull on him: in order to measure their trajectory, he had to lift his gaze.

And yet he entered churches with lowered eyes. He had long wondered why. Then he saw that he was going to die one day – that he was promised to the earth, not to the sky, kingdom of the stars. He probably sensed this – he had a feeling about it, which is to say he felt it in his flesh. And he responded, and prepared himself in some way: in the contemplation that churches inspired in him, there was always this idea of closeness with the earth – the idea of a subdued joy.

He entered churches as though they were his home, and maybe this was because they *were* his home: something always awaited him, but it was never God.

Time passed. In nests, even the birdsong unravelled. Mists wore thin against trees, rooftops, and telephone poles. Monsieur Bartolomé measured the wanings, the declining angle of years. At times, he felt that his steps, ripened by interminable wanderings in the city, were filling with loose sand. He would get lost and then – even in the heart of the city – he would have to reset his course by the compass of constellations. All the same, his head was of stubborn suns, his heart of straight grain, his body of roads ready to hatch. But in the parks, he walked walled in by ageing leaves. Light came over things like ferreting beams of stars. Everything fled. Were the mornings moored to sparrow hawks?

25

This, moreover, never ceased to amaze him: season followed season, and he was still on earth, alive. For a long time, he had thought he would not survive the child's disappearance. And now here he was, taking inventory of centuries, with scratches from the sun's claws marking the corners of his eyes, with foam and silver birchbark sprinkled through his hair. Pigeons used to come and sit on his shoulder. Now the world settled its pebbles on the back of his neck, that reed. From the light broken by the angles of streets, boutiques, faces, and cars, he retained only a little: life went by, life went by. The city shaped its race of stalls and noises; far off, the forest produced its hares.

What was at the summit of buildings? Empty space, attached to unimaginable birds. Yes, time was fleeing. Already Monsieur Bartolomé was not entirely of the world of human beings. He was the spectator fascinated by these miracles: the morning following the night, the leaves fallen and then risen again to the branches. And summer reappeared, and already it was Christmas again.

Once, he was prey to an infinitely violent emotion. His son had been gone for some years already. One day, while he was turning the soil in the little vegetable garden laid out in the yard, he discovered a metal box that had clearly been buried there by the child. With hands trembling, Monsieur Bartolomé unearthed the precious box: though its small metal body was gnawed by the fevers of the earth, it was nevertheless a survivor of its sojourn in shadows. As for the contents, they had not resisted – all that was left were mildewed scraps of a piece of paper from which the words had been erased, giving way to a resigned silence. The child's letter, that incredibly innocent witness of his ten years, had turned into a mockery of a manifesto. Monsieur Bartolomé had to struggle for a moment to release the box from an astonishing network of roots. *Like the remains of our bodies,* he thought then, *captive, held by force in the earth that seems otherwise mostly uninterested in the soul.*

But maybe, too, it was just that the soul did not carry enough weight. Just a mockery of a manifesto.

Everything he carried in his abdomen: this dog's soul, these living years sewn together with snow, these horses galloping towards the banks to drink the rivers, these otters finely carved by water and burrows, these pumas roving the grassy ways, these roots risen high only to flatten themselves in the light, these cities tuned to acts of the sun; all of this inner life escaped from him, day after day. Suns broke him with their dawns. His body suffered the crack of each gesture. What is the body of a man who searches without ever finding? The rags of a poor child.

For a long time, Monsieur Bartolomé had known that everything down here ends. He had nothing more pressed against his forehead than the laws of the sun. But inside him, worlds trembled: deep, strong valleys made of half-days and hope, which seemed so real they could be called births.

Fevers and agitation caused by his wounded memory created in him a curious phenomenon. Because of them he felt that he was living simultaneously within his body and separate from it. This body betrayed him: Monsieur Bartolomé expected it to do its job, but it was often more of an odd storekeeper, more preoccupied with the inventory of its organs than with their proper functioning. Monsieur Bartolomé would have liked to gain strength, to distill and then hurl suitable blood into his veins, to celebrate its mechanics, to tune his heart to the high song that, in his mind, wished to live. But this body did not know how to bend to requests. It did as it pleased, as though fulfilling the requests of some other than the one who ensured its subsistence. And so Monsieur Bartolomé was both beside and within himself, at once the observer and the subject of the trespasses, the contortions, and the brutalities this organism caused and whose torture he had no choice but to endure.

Perhaps it was for this reason that Monsieur Bartolomé felt more than ever like he was living beside life. Not in death, but outside of life, meaning as the spectator, observing in minute detail as things consumed themselves. As far back as he could remember, not a day had gone by when these words did not surface inside him: *All these people, how do they do it? How do they live as though they were unaware of their death at the end?* The world, as it was, was not his master. The body was. He had learned these things from it.

After the child's disappearance, dawn ceased to bathe the house in its new colours. In the park, trees were no longer moved by anything but the wind: birds seemed to have deserted the place. In the evening, sounds of neon signs, on cornices and on walls, rose up from the street. Monsieur Bartolomé would go out to the place where signs never died. Their rays exploded into the darkness dethroned. He walked beneath the white lance of an ad. His face was reflected in drops left by the rain. He observed cars left to the mercy of the city, sidewalks kneeling for pedestrians, light leaving establishments.

He possessed only a little, deep down: the night that closes late, the radio airborne on its antennae like gulls leaving the mast. His hair always leaning towards the gleaming sidewalk when it rained. A certain scent on his shirt when the seasons set off again. The curve in the staircase, the comfort and the melancholy of knowing that all is passing, crowned with contours.

What was he made of? He was born of a stone, building his days out of the wood of a few wrecked boats. But what was he made of? So little separated him from those stretched out beneath the earth, cheek to cheek with animal dens. Yes, what was Monsieur Bartolomé made of? Of pebbles, of bushes, and of a fearful heart when the windows grew dark. Of a little bit of day, and the things it embraces.

30

Out of each hour given to him, he made a kind of mirador, an observation post. He kept a lookout for a rain of burrows, a snow of straightened ink. He waited for a night when his son, somewhere below, would surely be admiring the stark, piercing beauty of the stars. But something – endlessly, and in spite of everything – called Monsieur Bartolomé back to his human task. He walked the streets, and the sun multiplied against the windowpanes threw itself at him like a thousand puppies playing.

He left the city more and more often. But he went less frequently to walk on the trails beneath the trees. He would hail a taxi, asking the driver to take him to where the last houses stood. Then he would stand still and observe the horizon. The light that he saw, far away between the hills, was different than the light he had left behind him. It was a light of the beginning of the world – in that place, the earth carried on its back only fish, green limes, and stones planning lives to come. The countryside laid itself down before this threshold of clarity. Behind Monsieur Bartolomé, the city was poised upon a pedestal.

Yes, something compelled him to escape the city. During the taxi ride, which the driver would likely have wished to be more animated, Monsieur Bartolomé did not speak at all. In the tank, the carbon burned, freed finally from its destiny as a fossil. The radio was on, bringing news of an agitated world: people were fighting here, people were thirsty there, planes were hurled at skyscrapers, a dictator fell.

Sometimes he was not content to stay standing still, looking far away. Once he was out of the car, he began to walk, advancing towards the horizon hemmed in by countryside. He took to dreaming the secular rhythm of tall trees. He crossed over wooden bridges, walked along gravel roads, and traversed fields bristling with prickles to arrive at the edge of a forest. He went to calculate the number of rings drawn in the wood of ancient cedars that had been cut down and left there by a peasant. He became part of the thoughtful tribe of slowness.

At the end of the day, he retraced his steps, hailed another taxi in the suburbs, and returned home. Night was already far along when he finally slid between the sheets.

One night, two sparrows came to the window. One said to him: "Wake up, the day is lengthening over the world, everything is breaking open and calling to you, come with me." Like a soul that will not leave the house though its occupant has departed, the other one stayed, its small body watchful in the curtain's nocturnal trembling.

2

# Night Worn Thin Against Their Hides

1

What was he searching for? A clearing, a place spun with space and light. A bright interval. A premonition of victory.

And if he looked for a clearing, it was because he suspected this much-desired victory was horizontal. Trees, buildings, masts, mountains, and other steeples shooting up into the air like so many arrows were not what inspired in him the most confidence. Instead, he looked to burrows, roots, horizon, roads, lakes, and prairies. Because he knew that he could lay himself down upon their backs, his forehead banded with clarity, and weigh the sun in his hand.

He left to go and live in the country, there where the trees were crowned with the same sky as the elm of long ago. He rented a small house nestled up against the forest, at the summit of a low mountain, not far from a village.

He had always been solitary, unobtrusive, and quiet, with little or no interest in unanimity. He took up very little space in the world. This did not change. And yet now he found that he needed all the space contained between his hand and the horizon, between his face and the first stars. Now the city ran him ragged with its heaping up of things, lights, gestures, and events. He was drowning in so much noisy proximity. He needed the territory suited to immeasurable silence emanating from his hands, his back, his hair, and his bones, that left him to lose itself in the unfurling of the countryside.

He chose to live in the country; it was the only place he had found where such amplitude was possible.

He bought a dog. Because his deepest complicities were mute:
they were born of his hand caressing a muzzle, of a paw placed
on his knee. He saw in the animal's gaze that unwavering con-
sent he had sought in vain in people's eyes: everything ends;
there is nothing we can do about it. He found in the dog's
company an explanation for the tragic beauty of the world. Oh!
How he loved to read in the eyes of his silent dog these words
like a handful of lights: "We will have passed through this life.
Is that not infinitely mysterious? Is it not of a sadness and a joy
without name?" It had taken him a long time to assent to these
words. He turned his face away, leaned his forehead against the
windowpane. The day lowered, and from far off, came sounds
of barking that Monsieur Bartolomé could understand.

Then there were the stars that came back each night as though to remind the earth of the miracle of things. These unsolved worlds, these rebel brightnesses scattered across the night, often kept him awake. For a long time, especially in his childhood when he was about the same age as his son when he disappeared, Monsieur Bartolomé had wished to fly to them aboard some vessel. But now it was he who sent for them, who welcomed suns into his space of shade. He envied their inexhaustible fate. He, too, would have liked to be the maker of mornings. He was with them as though among the lynx at the green hour of forests: together they waited for the coming day.

Fireflies, of course, came and went all the time, but it was only in the evening that they could be seen – only then that they began, in short, to truly exist. Did living begin, then, only at the precise instant when the contrast between self and the world was revealed? In adversity, in a sense? Whatever the case, Monsieur Bartolomé felt an affinity for the fireflies; he, too, felt that he began to live more fully when the light grew low, when the hours left him to his lone inner flame. What he retained from these extravagant insects was winged light, flown and then captured and cloistered in the belly like fire in headlights, a signal. But what was this sign emanating from the self, this coded flash, blinking like a signal fire in the dark? What was to be understood from these words in fire, these little contained blazes, suspended from the ropes of night? Because this flame, contradictory – captive and winged all at once – did not know what to do with its light. It stayed still for a moment as though timidly attached to the branches, hesitating between the dungeon of the grove and the torch of its own day. Then it reeled away, a lush staggering through the air, apparently electing for the darkness that soon swallowed it. Monsieur Bartolomé did not hold it back. He preferred the meditative match head reposing upon its wood, the simple daybreak that rose in its spattering.

6

He was born like this, with a brain inventing images. The world was multiple, stratified: beneath its surface was always another reality that came, unlooked for, to Monsieur Bartolomé. He did not immediately understand this other order of things. He had to decode it, like someone piecing together the fragments of an ancient vase broken by the centuries. He was the scribe of a scattered narrative, digging into the mud of omens. From this labour arose images, perceptions, and new worlds. Perhaps this was why existence seemed so strange to him, so full of mystery. Each thing, even the most ordinary pebble, concealed an undiscovered realm that Monsieur Bartolomé glimpsed by the light of a thin torch. He was born here, closer to a star than to humankind.

And so he always kept close to that which he sought to escape. Reality, the body, the most everyday objects – everything he could brush against was a substance that he split down the middle to extract something else, a new material. Thus, there were roads *in* the trees, churches *in* the flesh, words *in* the winds, a dream *in* his chair, larks *in* the dreams. A stone was never a stone, but a door whose design he studied in order to find the keyhole; and when, finally, the door turned on its hinges, it seemed to him that he found in this secret life – hidden until this moment – more reality than he had ever found in the life that contained it.

And it seemed to him that birds, too, were more than just birds. With one stroke of their wings, they left the earth to besiege the sky. This ordinary miracle, this enslavement of the air to the whims of birds, must surely hide a reality greater than them: you do not command the elements like that without having fabulous insight into existence. What did they know that we did not? What was concealed in those small musical bodies, flying over everything? Rain fell, valleys harboured flocks, hay hoisted itself up in the clearings. The world followed its course. Beneath those wings, suns carried countries home.

The backs of birds were palm of hands. And like hands, their wings enclosed something: globes, sextants, opera glasses? Monsieur Bartolomé crept close to the branches to gain a better understanding. He caught the weavers unaware, fabricators of fear and speed, colourists spattered with their own ink; singers, little airplanes of fabric, and claws. But he did not have access to their secret arithmetic. He went back to his notebooks, set down formidable theories in their pages.

It was an idea that had come early. When he was ten, or maybe eleven, he had chosen a profession: he wanted to build ladders. All the skies above had convinced him: how low the earth was! And up there, how full was the sky, with its suspended hippodromes, its roads, its dykes, its yokes, and galleons tied to their trajectories! He needed to reach these things. This is why Monsieur Bartolomé was what he was: a man with a dog's soul, worried and searching, an owl, a tree with thin bark, a bell, a green-winged teal's heart, a man rising up into vertigo. A builder of ladders. The reader, who has come to know him a little by now, might have thought Monsieur Bartolomé had a different profession. What? He is not a writer? It only seemed that way. He lived upon a mountain, a fistful of planets pegged in his skylight.

9

He learned to love foxes. It was not so much their moving beauty that affected him: other beasts made the forest irides-cent, perhaps with even more grace. But he kept watch for the fire that rushed through the ferns when the foxes passed. Because in earlier years he had forged deep friendships with brightnesses, and especially with the most fugitive ones. The red brightness of foxes, bound to their spines like the arrow to the wind, gave new life to his gestures. Even long after they had left, Monsieur Bartolomé reached his hands towards them, certain that he would find in their wake the hot fervour of stars. And yet – there was something beyond the bushy flame of their tails, beyond the wood burning to a cinder at their paws. He saw, on these luminous backs (so quickly seized by the copses), a certain brevity – akin to that which consumed him endlessly. Especially in the time since the child was no longer by his side, he loved the foxes for this: they reminded him to keep living.

Thus, he lived by the lone flame gathered at their muzzles. Once they had left, he lit the evening fires. A crow's wing lay folded on Monsieur Bartolomé's back. He preferred this meagre day to those of the city, stacked onto the tops of towers whose dawns promised nothing more than a heart hidden like a pit within the shadow of a fruit. Seated before his fire, he warmed the toes of his old shoes. In the morning, the wind escaped from the snare of foliage when the leaves had finally fallen asleep. Owls emerged from the bark. Fine clouds could be seen advancing like a little froth, like the dream of a wave:

56

the pond at the base of the mountain had begun to move the rowboat again. In its waters, fish wound round with light gave birth to new suns. Monsieur Bartolomé was now sure of this: other foxes would arrive, who would be the same age, and have the same gaze as his son.

Every year, autumn and then winter brought back their convoys of cold spells and burns.

At the end of their days together, when his dog dreamed of hay and new fields, Monsieur Bartolomé went to him as to a brother. He had, for his dog, fires like cities that he burned beneath the rooftops of stars in slow, slow lights. November came and the mountain put its trees, its animals, and its music to sleep. Leaves, released and then resurrected by the winds, confided to the valleys short chapters of otters and fish, now gone. The forest was full of sleep. Monsieur Bartolomé went back into the wood, his joy bound only to the thin backbone of the flame. Snow changed the world; he rested.

And it always came as though in a dream. Days followed days, time built its worlds, and suddenly the sky let slip that prodigious thing: snow. Snow, that light-footed dance slipping from the sky like sleep! He walked upon it, touched it like someone approaching a dream: with fingers numb from having stirred things up so, with feet heavy from so many steps taken upon the dry earth. But the snow had a brother, the cold, who wounded these gestures. Because of him, Monsieur Bartolomé no longer had access to the evidence of yesterday: suddenly, what was real was veiled by glass, a frost that burned his fingers.

But summer did return, and with it, the otters. It must have seemed to them that dogs were too hungry for the leash, and humans, too attached to their dogs. Monsieur Bartolomé heard the otters dive under the water and laugh to each other about him and his dog and their need to mingle muzzles with hands. They veered out into eddies, in the light corridors of the stream, practising the green dance stolen from the riverbanks. Monsieur Bartolomé left his work and went to watch them at their feast of river grass and water. When they saw him coming, they stretched out their necks. Perhaps they thought: *Here he is again, this curious animal. Will he use that strange thing again today, the thing he always carries with him?*

Because there was amazement in their eyes, a quiet astonishment that seemed to him to be caused by *that strange thing,* indeed, that is speech.

In the 1980s, Richard Leakey, palaeontologist and skilled fossil hunter, unearthed from Kenyan soil the remains of a young boy who had lived in East Africa one million, six hundred thousand years ago. This child, who would have been about twelve years old, was named Turkana Boy after the lake near which he was discovered. He and his fellow creatures are the dignified representatives of an important species of hominids called *Homo ergaster*. They were, on average, one metre, sixty centimetres tall, had large brains, small jaws, and opted resolutely for bipedism. Tall and resilient, they ran well – their long legs allowed them to cover great distances. They hunted large turkeys and invented new tools as well as the first weapons. According to many specialists in the field, it was they who gave rise to *Homo erectus* – so closely related to our direct ancestor, *Homo sapiens*. Whether or not this is true, the three species that are most closely related to us descended from them: *Homo heidelbergensis*, *Homo antecessor*, and *Homo neanderthalensis*, all of which appeared and disappeared within the last million years. And as we know, *Homo neanderthalensis* cohabited the earth with *Homo sapiens* a mere thirty thousand years ago.

Monsieur Bartolomé thought often of these things, which he had read here and there in various texts on the subject. He thought, of course, of Turkana Boy and the slight, oh-so-slight resemblance between his destiny and that of his son: this separation from his family at the age of twelve. Nearly two million years had passed between these two premature disappearances, and yet Monsieur Bartolomé could not help considering them as twin events. This made him faintly dizzy: at a time so far in the past that the mind had difficulty even conceiving of its existence, parents – beings still on the brink of human evolution but who had already surpassed the limited fate of animals, had lived through what he did now. Who knows what they had felt? Had the same emotions, those associated with incommensurable loss, broken their bodies, as they had his? Over and above morphological differences sculpted by the passage of millennia, was there something resembling a permanence of feeling, a sort of eternity for the murmuring of the heart, transmitted through the ages by the bonds of blood?

At night, his thoughts filled with such things.

Often, long after he had found sleep, a train would pass in the distance. The dog, too, was sensitive to the noise of the rails, even though this was stifled by the cushion of dusk upon the hills. Together they opened their eyes and then the animal left the carpet to come and rest his muzzle, still warm from the idleness of afternoon, upon the pillow. Monsieur Bartolomé could almost hear him say: "Listen with me to the train growing distant. Because, if we do not, who else will hear its moan?" It was as though he was measuring all the desolation that would follow on the inexorable route of the rails, as though he sympathized with the terrible destiny of the engine launched into the night of the world. The dog's silhouette was all that could be made out, cut from the half-dark of the room by the moon. And yet, in his eyes shone a light that bore into the dimness. His master got up, went to the window to peer out at the hill. He could never make out anything but a bracelet of deep ink. He imagined the train, plunging into this clay, the beam of its locomotive the only headlight. It was a brightness like a spade – like the eye of the dog when he joined his night to that of Monsieur Bartolomé.

He returned to bed. He dreamed. And in his dream, his son played beneath a tree, silent as ever.

All along the length of the rivers, he and the herons observed one another. The great birds walked slowly, folding and then unfolding their long dreamer's legs, searching the water for a meal or the outline of a meditation. He did the same, lengthening his steps in reverie along the bank. Often the rain showed up, lured by the cloth of greyness thrown over their shoulders. At a certain moment the herons would freeze, suddenly halting their advance between the stones cloaked in algae: a memory, you might have said, had resurfaced, removing them from themselves for three or four seconds – the time it takes for remembrance to uproot the great tree of the present. Then they would fly away, for no apparent reason: there was nothing, no noise, no sudden fright nor particular attraction in the air to justify this flight. They simply left. Could it be that they responded to the call of memory? Who would know their next appointments? Monsieur Bartolomé turned up his collar and returned to his momentarily interrupted train of thought. All around him, motionless, the big trees also seemed to ruminate. An elm was planted there. Monsieur Bartolomé observed it for a long moment.

The world was inexplicable, and yet, on certain days, Monsieur Bartolomé understood many things. Few mysteries could not be unravelled through his science; worlds were caught in his eyes, and he christened these worlds with names. He drank from the rains as though from drainpipes, taught them which passages to follow, prepared riverbeds that he had swindled from rowboats to receive their runoff. The rivers, too, were tributaries of his veins, and the beats of his heart were a series of islands as are beans in a pod. And few mysteries could not be unravelled through his science, because he translated the precise dedication of the sun with ease. The world was inexplicable, but something of it carved out a path in Monsieur Bartolomé.

He walked in each evening. It was there that his steps always began. You might have said that they aligned themselves with things of the moment: the light spilling over the windowpane, the grasses standing straight again now that the wind had grown quiet. He became that drifting surveyor, marking out hills, inventorying contrasts, contours, aspects, angles – all that the day had left behind. His steps were just like chapels, spaces we enter in silence. While he waited for the dawn, he placed them on roads that seemed risen to meet him. A city or a village sometimes captured and enclosed them in its rolling swells. But suns called them back each time, constellated with baby swallows. How to say it? The morning fell into his traps.

Did the earth and its sky stop here, right out in front, just above, so close you could almost touch the buckles, the clasps, the overflows, and the star machines? Of course, Monsieur Bartolomé knew the earth to be seated like a chair. He knew the mysterious dance of the worm beneath her, and above her, he knew the moon who constructs the tides. He knew the world shaping its swift passage of people and landscapes in relief, and at midnight, he knew the compact cave of its sky. What else did he know? When it grew very late, his fire closed down and the stags came near the branches to eat stars. Their gaze met Monsieur Bartolomé's, but the stags walked on towards the dawn with the indifference of stones. But did the world stop here, right out in front, just above, so close?

Something always lay in wait for him, something he did not recognize that held him by the shoulders, this gallows in the middle of himself. He searched out the face, the name, and the age of this thing, but he had his steps as sole gestures, set down in the shadows erased by the dawns. Still he searched: he studied the heights and wished for attics to sprout from the tops of ladders. But what were fish made of? Of lost islands and boats carried off by distracted lighthouses. But what did the snow dream of? Of the day, for she is its damaged sister in the world.

It wasn't that he forgot the child. But with time, the image of him faded and left in its place something infinitely more difficult to describe, with only the vaguest of outlines: an emotion, maybe the dream of this image. And it was not that the emotion was any less strong than the image it arose from. Only, at the same time that he was endlessly stalking an elusive sky within himself, Monsieur Bartolomé lived among things of the world and fed himself, in a certain way, with their very materiality. It was as though he, who was so invisibly *inhabited*, needed to convince himself of his own reality by touching the perimeter of things, by experiencing through his senses the indisputable proof of their existence.

Also, perhaps in order to preserve a definite image of his son, he had made a little garden in the yard of his small house (because Monsieur Bartolomé had never forgotten his discovery of the small metal box buried among the kohlrabi). In August, he bent over the full-grown beans. He examined their skins that, for the entire summer, had been preparing the little train of beans lying within. All along the spines and on the bellies, as well, there was this slight wound whose thin scar suggested unreal images: the blade of a knife had slid along here, and inside this sort of glove that is the pod, a life had been inserted. When he in turn opened this pod, he always felt that he was interrupting a dream: something mythical ceased. What was it that he disturbed? A train's rapid course challenging the closed horizon?

21

At the end of the slope near the house, at the foot of the mountain, was a pond.

Each summer a couple of loons nested on the bank, and their tearing song was carried to him while he lingered under the trees in the evening. It was a cry that spoke of all the strangeness of living: these houses, these cars, these mountains, these people, all this space ... who put this here? In June, a little one was born, who balanced on its mother's back for a time – astonished lifeboat atop its silent, stately vessel. From then on, the song that rose up from the bank was not quite the same as before – the mystery and the formidable melancholy contained within it had grown even deeper. Monsieur Bartolomé thought of his son, of the years when he was still with him in the house in the city; he thought of the child's slight anxiety at times when joy was not strong enough.

What Monsieur Bartolomé loved about the night was its lights: spume, lamps, birches, shop windows, street lamps, moon, windowpanes, fires, snow, stars, and fireflies. All these vigils, these miniscule mornings that refused to surrender. Night was a promise held fast by the first ribbons of dawn. Moorings of waiting and dreams were tied to the full hours of shadows after midnight. Sometimes periods of wakefulness kept a tight rein on his step. One morning, three grey wolves arrived, the night worn thin against their hides.

The rain continued to fascinate him. Aside from his need for contact with reality, with objects and all things tangible, this was one of the rare things from his past that had stayed with him: his deep curiosity about the rain. Almost all rains were sad. And yet, he considered them to be irreplaceable companions, perhaps because they imprinted flowers and branches with the same familiar movement he drew with his body each time he leaned towards the earth.

Storms, at times, would graft themselves to daybreak and disguise it as evening. The rain descended, weighing down the animals' long wait in its passage. With muzzles raised, they kept watch for the precious metal of the sun. You might have said that the world was hindered in its profession as a carousel: ropes of rain tethered it to the stars that stopped in their course and halted the hoop of its rotation. But all these forces joined in vain: in the end, the light always broke through. The morning rolled out its clearing.

When the rain stopped, the leaves became little boats that hung from the shoulders of the bushes. Monsieur Bartolomé went out; he walked in the forest. He went like the ferns, keeping watch for the passage of animals that dissolved into the paths. In places where the path turned, he waited for something, as you might wait for a road and find beneath your feet only a forest unfolding itself, and unfolding its wildcats and endless green.

He knew nothing of the twilight: four o'clock came and suddenly he had to believe in tomorrow. Time passed. Was his hair reminded of its snowy vocation? Time passed, and far off in the distance, suns were crushed in the mills.

The pond had become an important part of his solitary life. He had not intended this – it just was. It was for this pond that the light began, and for its quenched stags, its museum of stags. The pond was made of a young dog running to rescue old sticks. Of forests hung from the oar. Of ducks placed on their palms, the sun in their wings. Of fish swimming like bright coins. At the end of full hours, when the leaves were half-quieted, soft sounds rose up from its surface and its banks. Monsieur Bartolomé opened his window and listened. Once, he heard the voice of his son. Or was it just the curtain, come to brush across the loaf of bread on his table?

Because it seemed that the faint image of the child was reflected in the water of the pond. And sometimes it was more than just an image: you would have said the child himself was there, lying amidst the rushes. Only the lapping of the waves disturbed the calm of his face. But what was this agitation in the evening that scratched at the water so? Was it his young hair combing through the slow work of the hours? The wind blowing over the fish? The mute gesture of the rowboat, dreaming there at the end of the pond? None could say. But it seemed that the child was sleeping in the years, rocked by the supple song of the rushes.

It was a ritual, almost a mass: every morning, he went to undo the calm of the pond. He threw a stone at the surface, then another, and still more. The disturbance in the water brought him some comfort. He saw in it a victory over the indifference of things. Was the prayer of the believer, thrown at the smooth face of the sky, aimed at anything other than this? The small waves caused by his stones came to brush against new lights. In this way, thick liquids and precious jewels formed upon the pond's surface: Monsieur Bartolomé was strong, and rich. He lingered a moment in the grasses. From that point on, nothing was still. Something had been broken. This was the whole of his religion: he liked to believe that once it had been moved by his gestures, the sky, or its reflection, remained turned towards him, vibrating.

Daybreak often found him out fishing. But he never caught any. Leaning his chest over the edge of the rowboat, he watched them instead, tirelessly. How did they do it? He searched their scales for the key to their mystery. But maybe this was not enough. Maybe he should have questioned the day as well, who is closest to them – for what are fish without light? Ships gone under, all signals extinguished, floating down sideways. Still he could see them slipping between the draperies of the water with fire upon their flanks, thrown like sharpened knives. The pond emerged unharmed from this carnage: behind them, the wound closed up and the liquid tissue forgave, healed over just as quickly. These questions came to his mind: where do fish come from, besides from the shadows of silt? Where do they go, elusive and gleaming? And most of all, how do they do it, these beings who are so different from us, to leave behind only so brief a wound?

Very early in the morning, the windows were snagged in the sun's net and otters were born in the folds of rivers. At midday, the shade rose and went to drink from corollas. The day passed like this until it closed the eyes of animals in their burrows. At twilight, Monsieur Bartolomé lingered there, leaning over the threshold of these burrows with one ear cocked. But neither voice nor movement reached him: in hollows of the earth, animals slept like hands inside gloves.

His dog died. Monsieur Bartolomé found him one afternoon, lying in the grasses, his muzzle floured with age, his hazel eyes closed on the world forever. And yet, what a glow had burned behind the thin hedge of his eyelids! The five-o'clock light fell upon the animal's blond and gently curved back, colouring it gold. A gentle breath of air came over this round loaf, still warm, and extinguished the last lights that had lived in this body only moments before. A dragonfly alighted on the dog's forehead. Bent over the motionless body of his old companion, Monsieur Bartolomé slowly brought his hand close enough to touch the insect's wings with his fingertips, and the dragonfly did nothing to prevent him. He wanted to see in this a sign: of goodness, faithfulness, and intelligence lingering for a moment, even beyond death.

The dog had lived for nearly twenty years beside his master. Three things had marked this exceptionally long existence. Throughout these years, among so many things observed, his brown gaze had fallen on only a few humans, when they crossed his path in the neighbouring village. At night, the man who accompanied him everywhere on this earth got up to watch the rain. And above all, above everything, each day for twenty years, he had seen in this same man's eyes, this ageing writer always bent over his notebooks, the calm and thoughtful face of a twelve-year-old child.

Something had burrowed, burrowed into him still. Now, the otters, the badgers, and the prairie dogs had his name written on their flanks. Clasping faded suns in their paws, they got caught in his steps. Monsieur Bartolomé grew old. An earthen den enclosed him in its inventory of shadows. He placed a few things there: a well-loved tree, a narrow path, a pond through the hours, a small garden. Only a few things. He carried lanterns, and winds came to blow them out. He lit them again with sparks that spilled from stones. He knew insects decorated with wings and the sunset, and pheasants preparing endings. Were the days so shallow? His fires disappeared into a thousand nights. At the bend in the footpath, the nimble pages of the years were turning. The wind unfurled furtive cardinal points where nests lay in fountain beds. But where did this subterranean corridor of his flesh lead, towards which abode shaken by the branches? Nothing was more full of mystery than the passage into old age.

He had a dream. In the small yard of the house of long ago, his son hung by his knees from the lowest branch of the elm, upside down and smiling, absorbed in some child's game. Above the tree, the sky stretched out as far as the eye could see, full of the boy's silence. The stillness of this sky was disturbed only by the movement of the leaves, brightened where the sun had come to toss minuscule pieces of day. You would have said, then, that the branches were moving ahead through the immensity, pushed forward by the luminous gesture stationed there at the top of the tree. This impression – of a fabulous vessel made of wood and bark – was heightened by the central image of the trunk, emerging from the leafy hold like a mast to plant itself in that other sky that is the earth. But when he saw this extraordinary upside-down structure that seemed to be readying itself to take the other side of the world by storm, Monsieur Bartolomé was struck by one thing above all others: the sole passenger (which seemed to suggest that he was also the captain, leaning over some marine map, dreaming perhaps of conquests and prodigious advances) was his own son.

Monsieur Bartolomé awoke. Night covered the world still. Through the open window, he could hear the forest, lightly stirred by the breeze. This sound mingled with the lapping of the pond, so closely that it seemed the branches sheltered a solitary and tireless rower, making his way through the vast aerial domain of shadows.

He knew, then, that the sea was calling him.

# 3

# A Seahorse Ballet

He left the mountain, the fields, the trees, and the animals that he had lived close to for so long, and went to live by the sea. Here, on this rough-edged shore, where wind and waves came to coarsely shape the coast, a fisherman let him a small solitary house for next to nothing. It was basic but comfortable. This suited him – it corresponded to the urgent need he felt now for a state of being that was stripped bare. Before him, the sea also met this need, with its large tarpaulin that seemed to mimic the nakedness of the skies, and despite the fact that it concealed a world of unfathomable complexity within the folds of its fluid garment.

And was this not precisely the image of what Monsieur Bartolomé had always been: a man naked, unrough – meaning alone, without the rugged coat that life in society forms over the soul as a result of repeatedly brushing against that tormented country of the other? But like the sea, Monsieur Bartolomé was also an agitated man, his very body traversed by currents and whirlpools sometimes fearsome, inhabited by strange creatures, more at home in silt than on the beds of light formed by the sun in the high belly of the waves. Inside Monsieur Bartolomé there rested silent vessels, sunken long before but still recalling the storms that had lost them.

It was this part of himself that pushed him forward; this part that left the imprint of the primordial movement of his existence, and forced him, ceaselessly, to press his steps upon the world; to search, and search still more. Did the body take sustenance, then, from this mysterious, painful life, as though responding to the call from that other part of being which is the soul – yes, that sky tangled in every person, and so closely related, here, to the ocean, from which it was separated by no more than the thin thread of the horizon.

2

In his book of essays entitled *The Sea*, Jules Michelet writes: "Great, very great, is the difference between the two elements: the Earth is mute and the Ocean speaks. The Ocean is a voice. It speaks to the distant stars … It speaks to the Earth and to the shores, replying to the echoes that reply again; by turns plaintive, or threatening, it groans or sighs. It speaks to human beings in particular. As it is the fecund womb in which creation began and still continues, it has creation's living eloquence; it is Life speaking to Life. The millions, the countless myriads of beings to which it gives birth, these are its words. That milky Sea from which they come, even before they are formed, while yet white and foaming – speaks. All of this together, intertwined, this is the great voice of the Ocean."

Monsieur Bartolomé had never found anything beneath the trees and between the hills but silence, or a variation on silence: the wind tossing the leaves, the step, and the cry of animals mixing with the felted night, the passage of stones tumbling from the incline, conceded to valleys by the mountain, with rain come to nail a bit of sky to the earth, and then rising again with the sky in its diaphanous chariots. A silence of the organs, lifted from the great body of the earth. This language of silence had served him well. But now a new voice was raised, one that Monsieur Bartolomé had to heed, a voice from the sea and thus, perhaps, closer to life than all the other ones that had been heard since the dawn of time.

He understood one thing. This large receptacle of life, this first journeying place of existence, this great workroom of fertility – this was the belly of which the poets spoke. The world had its encampment here. What Monsieur Bartolomé heard when he stood on the strand, was that not the voice of the beginning, of all beginnings? And was he not now the child about to be born from the great belly of the world?

3

The fisherman left him a boat as well, old but solid enough to tackle the ocean's ordinary riots. And so each day, Monsieur Bartolomé went out upon the sea. He stopped rowing at the moment when his house, far off on the deserted shore, was reduced to the size of a tiny box. Tossed by the waves, he squinted his eyes and observed this for a moment. *This house is a metal box, like the one my son buried in the garden,* he sometimes thought. *And I am in the box like the message I once found: a mute letter, wordless from now on, grown quiet perhaps in order to leave room for the voice of something greater than the self.*

He would drop anchor then, and stay there for long hours, listening to what the ocean had to say.

4

As time went by, salt collected and dried on the rowboat until
its sides were covered with a tenacious layer of sediment. After
a few months, Monsieur Bartolomé would have to overturn the
vessel on the shore and with the point of his knife scrape away
the stony suit draped over the old planks by the waves. It was
usually at night, or late in the evening, when he set about this
arduous task. His age hardly permitted the effort it demanded,
but at least the absence of the raging sun helped.

Once, as midnight approached and while the blade of his
instrument came and went at a good rhythm over the prow, he
lifted his eyes to the firmament. Beneath the action of the knife,
the salt, which just a second before had been stuck to the wood,
spattered the night. Showers of light filled the air, formed from
hundreds of tiny diamonds, scattered as though by some seed
sower. Struck by this image, Monsieur Bartolomé paused in his
work. Then he went back to his task, slowly, not without tast-
ing the nameless joy that he felt rising within him. Because it
seemed to him that not only was he creating stars – he was also
touching them with his hand.

Indeed, what were the stars made of? Of salt, sawdust of the sea. The ocean took on the task of making wood for those incandescent trees that are the distant stars. Likewise, the ocean took care of installing them in the sky: was it not true that the clouds were escaped from ocean swells that had loosed their hold for a moment? The whole sky was formed in this way: it was never anything but the fruit of the earth's embrace.

When he walked along the beach, Monsieur Bartolomé turned this thought over in his mind: *What if, in fact, the sky itself was a tree, the great family tree of all things, its roots drawing strength from the sea?* Images of the rain, which he watched through the window at midnight, were always woven into his thoughts. Yes, the sky in those hours resembled the belly of whales. And the water that fell from it tasted of salt, of tears, of the wood of elm trees and of first sorrows.

6

At low tide, exposed suddenly from beneath the sand where they had found refuge, small crabs appeared and began to survey the beach. Visibly disoriented, they searched, without much success, for the shortest path to the ocean that had left them behind so offhandedly. In just an hour or two, their usual pasture of water had been mysteriously transformed. It was as though, stunned by the fact that the holes where they had fallen asleep just a little while ago were now nearly dry, they suddenly became prisoners, but prisoners behind strange bars – made of sand, space, and open air.

In the end, low tide was no more than a brief detention, a warning shot: from now on, the crabs would do better to stop their loitering in these precarious zones where the moon still had such clear authority over the waters. For the moment, there was nothing to do but wait, wait and pace. Maybe their steps would lead them to a door that opened onto the ocean.

Monsieur Bartolomé often lingered to examine them with the end of his stick, these little fallen knights thrown from their mounts. Equipped with only their armour and pincers, they threatened him with this sort of halberd that was an extension of their arms, colliding vainly with empty space at each thrust. In the end, the animal abdicated.

It withdrew wisely, sidling away, still holding the gaze of its adversary. Monsieur Bartolomé observed all this without a word. He returned to his reverie, to his cage of sand, space, and open air.

The beach stretched away on either side of the house. Whether setting out to the left or to the right, it was a long way before the cliff – suddenly advancing to the water as though to get a drink – blocked the walker's progress with its great body. At that point, you had to content yourself with retracing your steps, since the rock face, abrupt as a tower, was insurmountable. The wall standing there let nothing distract it: in its stone dignity, its high forehead watching the ocean closely, it would not be diverted from its ancient role. This geological lighthouse, sculpted by the air and the water for the exclusive use of the waves crashing up against its foot, was entirely devoted to its shepherd's task.

Sometimes, other walkers left traces of their steps on the sand. Once the walkers were gone, Monsieur Bartolomé added his own footprints to theirs. He thought that in all his life this was perhaps the closest intercourse he had had with his fellows. Even during his time in the big city long ago, despite the fact that he was surrounded by thousands of other human beings, he had never felt truly close to them. But today, it seemed to him that he retained something from the footprints he followed, so briefly imprinted upon the shore. In his mind, he saw again the image of his son. He said in a low voice: "Will I have been good only for understanding the essence of things, only for grasping the reflection, the memory of them?" Permeated by this idea, he reached the cliff. Silent and haughty, her face turned towards the distance, she pushed him away with her large rock hand.

8

In the thickest part of the night, the moon was a ship's hold. A sun wished to pierce its metal. Beneath this iron day, the sea leaned over, set up pitchings and tossings to bring the tides to life. Ships passed on the horizon, hesitating between two plains, one fluid and full of fish, the other premeditating winds and air-plane routes. But in the end, their signal fires always scraped the backs of the blue whales. Prows walked on the water. The sea prevailed over the sky.

Sometimes, too, just before dawn, humbler boats came near, pushing a few waves onto the shore as they passed. The last bits of night were seated on the rails. Above the muffled motors, worn out in advance by a hard day's fishing, gulls lonely for sleep wheeled like lilies whose stems were too frail. In their flight was some of the disorder of hands ruled by love: a fever gloved it, arranged in slow tendernesses by the prospect of a satisfied hunger.

The fabric of the sky was crimson above all this.

The ocean advanced, receded. It hesitated. Or perhaps it was the earth, rather, that stood up straight, imitating its own flowers. In any case, something toppled, spilling an excess of angles: the world, for a time, transcribed the flat page of the sky. It was the tides and their continual work of recapitulation: a marsh marigold of light that was never fully realized proceeded from these progressions, these obstinate withdrawals. The tides moved things back and forth ceaselessly, sliding the seat out from under them as though to remind Monsieur Bartolomé of his inescapable fate of movement, of growing closer, of distancing, and perhaps above all, of precariousness.

The azure skies also had their swaying. Were not the twilight and then the dawn an aerial version of the sort of deliberation that moved the sea? This hesitation at the edge of a day, these oscillating fields that are the end and the beginning of light, translated for Monsieur Bartolomé the idea that we are defined by our adversaries, or at least by our counterparts. Through the succession of days and nights, the ebb and flow, the ocean, the sky, and the earth studied each other. At the heart of the most elementary reality of the world, they tried to learn about each other. Ten thousand, a hundred thousand generations of stones, waves, and clouds visiting each other faithfully had not been enough for them to come to know one another.

After leaving the beach and walking a little ways along the cliff, you would come to a lighthouse. The old red-and-white building stood on a tongue of land that stretched far out into the ocean. It kept watch for boats that, seen from this promontory, seemed to be born mysteriously at the summit of high waves. Or perhaps this was no mystery after all. From the mix of water and light projected onto the night, from this alchemy resulted a simple lineage: out there, vessels *saw the light of day*, quite literally. On board, a birth took place; on mildewed ropes and in streaming cabins a spring began. With the cape in sight on maps, tiller lifted the captain filling a cup of coffee on deck, the sailors finally relaxed their fingers where they had been clutching the sides of bunks too tightly. The lantern wick was lowered. Hope, or perhaps faith, returned to hearts, minds, and bodies, too.

Monsieur Bartolomé liked to go out on the sea in the rain. Because it seemed to him then that the sea was everywhere. With its whole cheek leaning over, the sky poured out dreams of fish. The ocean gathered them up. Monsieur Bartolomé liked to find himself in the middle of this; he liked to have this shimmering, nacreous jaw close over the boat as though over a pearl.

He thought of his son, of his games beneath the great elm. Mingled with the shade of the tree, the child probably felt something similar to what his father felt now: a feeling of imprisonment, confinement, but in a place that opens onto a realm, since the only ramparts that surround it are like arms. An embrace. Words pronounced long ago came back to him: "I was the father of an island." Because indeed, the well-loved tree had enclosed the child in the manner of waves. But what he felt even more, now, was that a sort of filiation, made from the zeal of sap, from the strange reverie of bark, and from the creative logic of the sea, had established itself between Monsieur Bartolomé, his son, and the ocean.

Later the rain stopped. The horizon had toyed with its hinge and opened the world again. The oars bit into waves, and then the boat was pulled onto the sand, tied to the post with a rough rope. A cormorant slept upon the roof of the house, its feathers smoothed by the evening wind.

Aside from crabs, other animals tossed up on shore by the waters roused his curiosity – some even stirred him deeply. Crustaceans were among these. Monsieur Bartolomé had certainly pored over the anatomy of these little creatures before. But never before this day had he considered with such acuity the extraordinary advantage of their composition. Each time he ousted one from its sand hole to examine it, it made his imagination run wild, and solicited his admiration – which was almost jealousy. How he envied them! Because these creatures, so ungraceful, seemingly so unfavoured by nature, possessed in their very constitution something that Monsieur Bartolomé did not have in his, and that he wished to find there. It was the little calcareous house enveloping their tender bodies that evoked in him this keen emotion. Yes, this shell, far more than a simple exoskeleton lending shape and structure to a body, a mould where silky fabric came to lean as though against a supporting wall – this shell was a shelter. And while Monsieur Bartolomé rubbed his thumb across the remarkable patina, he murmured: "Happy are those on this earth who find a refuge in their own flesh. In that secure place, they can rest their limbs, sore from journeys and quests. The heart can lie down there like the coyote on the warm straw of a solar ray. Peace can enter."

Perhaps we never completely leave the places where love has filled us with its grace. Thinking back, no doubt, on the small yard behind his house in the city and his very first vegetable garden, Monsieur Bartolomé liked to imagine the beach as a fertile plot where the seeds of some primordial, elementary food were planted. Crustaceans reinforced this imagery for him. And oh, when he exhumed these little living cases, how he saw once again the metal box buried by the child so long ago! What new letter, what story was consigned to the depths this time by the ocean's stormy hand? With the edge of a pebble, he lifted the lid of mussels, oysters, and scallops. Lips confessed a world. An island was stretched out in these stone cradles. Sea within sea, rain upon rain, a body floated there, as though poured out, spilled perhaps from the streaming runoff of a tear, promised to a higher life, waiting for either a pearl or a seahorse ballet, or maybe the glide of a whale. Gently, Monsieur Bartolomé closed the shell again, put this little jewel case back down upon the soaked sand, returning to its bed the silence whose night he had cracked open with his hand.

In the open sea, they arrived in groups, cattle looming up from the deep, and combed with their giant baleen the few hundred metres of water sown with the richest fodder: plankton. Krill, diatoms, protozoa, eggs, larvae, molluscs of all shapes and sizes, thousands of animal and plant species, a whole errant life teemed there, offered up to the abyssal appetite of the whales.

Monsieur Bartolomé watched them as they slowly glided around the rowboat, breathing spray here and there from their blowholes, splashing and greeting him, you might have said, with their fins or their tails standing straight upon the water like the sails of an ancient galley. He always felt a sort of rapture at the sight of these animals. Sometimes, when the sea was calm, he dove in to meet them. As though to warn each other of the approach of this tiny newcomer, some of them sounded their familiar song, muted by the ocean's thick walls and at the same time strangely echoed by these, sometimes for dozens of kilometres around.

To him, the whales held a formidable contradiction: their very size rendered them almost unreal. They were so big that they tended, in the mind, towards non-existence. It was too much to comprehend. Landscapes, skyscrapers, oceans, and machines could be oversized – that was graspable. But for a living being to have such close ties with a mountain? No, that defied reason. It was this, this infinitely tangible miracle, that so fascinated Monsieur Bartolomé: that the breast of mountains could vibrate to the rhythm of a beating heart, that they could breathe, move, and even float. What was more: that they could sing.

15

One day, he made a grisly discovery. The body of a drowned man, pulled from the grip of silt by deep currents, had washed up on shore. Thus this body, even after death, had been animated by some kind of ultimate life: dark forces had given it the order to rise, to stand up and return to solid ground, in a sort of march towards its final destination, a return to its point of departure. A bizarre march, and violent, guided by the dirty gleam reflected in fish eyes, by the erratic paths of jellyfish; a march punctuated by the turbulence of the water.

The body was still relatively intact. The man had clearly only been under for a matter of hours, or at most a few days. Monsieur Bartolomé decided that he had to finish the job begun by the sea. He resolved to burn the remains.

It was disturbing to see the body being consumed. As soon as the flames had begun their work, it folded inward in a strange convulsion, returning, you might say, to the position of an embryo in its mother's womb. But it was a reverse birth: here, rather than coming loose from the earth, the body embraced it, gave back its substance and humours. Within the fire's empire, the flesh smoked and withered like a worn shirt. Then the carcass blackened and broke, and he could see the source of the marrow dry up, the entrails boiling in the pot of the abdomen. Monsieur Bartolomé watched the frozen smile of the dead form slowly, the smile that comes when the skin of the face is stripped away by the great disrober that is death. He saw the hands stripping off their cover of flesh. He thought: *Whose was the last face touched by these hands?* Later, when the body was

103

almost entirely devoured, he said to himself: "In the end, which of these two realities – life or death – will have consumed this man more fully?"

Evening came, and then the night. But Monsieur Bartolomé did not go home, preferring to stay on the beach mulling over these things. And he was probably reluctant to extinguish the fire that was, it seemed to him, the last manifestation of the life of this man who had been cast yesterday upon the shores of the world. In the end, the dawn broke, and saw to taking down this lamp.

The fire, always. In the evening, after cooking his meal over a few coals, Monsieur Bartolomé sat down right next to it and warmed his big boots on the red-hot stones. He lifted his gaze to see the day slowly decline. Then the stars came out and their wicks brightened the great scarf of night, and once again, he ate in the company of his old friends. The fire, always.

Although it was common enough for Monsieur Bartolomé to speak aloud during the day, he was almost always silent once darkness had descended. It was not that he lacked things to say to himself. Nor was he short on words. Writers, it's true, exhibit layers of impoverishment. A part of them is like the hay in the fleeting hours of summer's end: emptied of its grain, ever distracted by suns. Only, in their case, words come to combat these shortages of being. But how to say it? Once evening came, though they still ripened inside Monsieur Bartolomé, his words stopped their blossoming all at once and refused to take shape, to flower upon the field of his tongue. In the evening, he was like the owl in its night of feathers and bark, preferring the silence of the shadows to the harsh sound of talk.

It was in these moments that he was most filled with this incredibly strong feeling that had inhabited him his whole life: the feeling of waiting. In silence, maybe because he felt it would have to come on velvet feet, Monsieur Bartolomé waited for something, some advent, and almost an entire life had not been enough to teach him what. The return of his son? He could not reasonably expect such a thing, not now. But these days, while the years brought him unrelentingly closer to death, he knew, at least, that this waiting had a name. It was called hope, precisely because it was always from the night that it arose.

The ocean was nothing like a pond. To disturb it, a stone would certainly not suffice. In fact, for that, the ocean needed no help from the negligible intervention of humans. As though arising from deep within, rages shook it, wounding its sides, allowing glimpses of its inner life: even in the middle of the day, nights would rise to its surface, fringed with tatters of light left by the passage of foam that might suggest – as in a kind of prayer – a bygone calm. The film of great shipwrecks rolled in reverse: from the depths rose the remains of hulls, rudders, cabins, and stern posts, which furious whirlpools rounded up and reorganized in their fatal way. At their command, new and terrifying ships came back to life and began to sail this heaving sea. You could just make out the faces of ravaged sailors on board, their eyes eaten away by the water, gusts of wind streaming through their long skeletal bodies. All this was the ailing memory of the sea, awoken, perhaps, by the floodlight of a new lighthouse – it was the pain of a sabre suddenly licking an ancient wound.

Beneath the boat, threatening mouths gaped open. At first, when he was surprised on the open sea by one of these gales, Monsieur Bartolomé had been stricken with terror. His body beaten by winds, his hands white, his big boots full of frothing water, his eyes dilated, he stared in horror at the chasms dug by the waves and had seen, more than once, his death approaching. Then, after some months had passed, he stopped being afraid. He got used to these tremendous squalls that resembled, in their effervescence, the turbulence – sometimes so great! – of human destiny.

18

His death. A small voice inside reminded him of it. Wherever he was, he heard it speak to him, and this is what it said: "Who would you be today if you knew your death was imminent? The walker aligning his walk with the lights, the wildcat without a dream in its belly, its ear filled up with shelter? Or the fearful man, murmuring these words to himself: 'What have you done with the world, what have you done with your human heart? How many days were betrayed by your orders, and how much did you get for them? And the shadows that you burned, what wrongs did they commit, and the night, why was she rejected by your eyes, strangled in her column of stars?' "

At times, he was inhabited by a strange impression. It was as though death was practising on him. He felt himself decline, his whole body bending low, his legs refusing to carry him any farther. Someone was selling off his steps. But this premonition of death was useful to him: it allowed him to realize that, when his day came, he would not be afraid. A stray dog might come near, and Monsieur Bartolomé would put his hand on the moist muzzle. A question would be in the eyes of the animal: "What made you a good inhabitant of the earth?" And the response would be something like this: "Who can say, aside from the evenings when they switch off the birds?" No, he would not know quite how to answer this question. But he would not be afraid.

He also thought: *I want to live my death. I hope it warns me – that it does not take me by surprise, while my back is turned, in my sleep, or by some sudden failure of the body.* He made it promise him one last look at things, deep, slow, the most attentive of gazes – the last one. He claimed his right to say goodbye to this terrible beautiful world that he would most certainly never see again. He would not let his death forget this promise, and this is why from that moment on not an hour passed when he did not call to it and question it, reminding it of the sort of pact they had made so long ago: yes, he would wait for it, but it also had to wait for him. This was his way of making sure that it did not have the last word. This seemed to suit death, and Monsieur Bartolomé could not have said why.

One night, he witnessed a horrifying storm. When the roar of
the wind tore him from his sleep, he came to the window to
behold the exceptional fury of the elements. The sea stood up
before him, foaming, torn by lightning bolts, opening terrifying
mouths that gobbled up the dense, hard, black rains unleashed
by the sky like hate. Because the sky, offended and vengeful,
took part in this ire – the bristling waves, having risen to heights
beyond their strict domain, must have violated some celestial
intimacy. Even the earth got involved, requisitioning its valleys
and prairies to reflect and scatter the thunder's terrible echo.
The whole world was contorted.

This lasted all night. Then, like a referee, the dawn stepped
in, and the combatants calmed down, shot each other a few
final dark looks, and declared an end to the war of attrition that
had broken out that night, for a reason now forgotten.

When he went out to the beach, Monsieur Bartolomé found
astonishing structures curiously aligned along the border of the
ocean and the earth – genuine sandcastles erected and then
abandoned there by furious waters, wind, and rain. These were
magnificent constructions placed there by an expert hand –
which, sadly, the tide already threatened to annihilate. Before
it did its work, Monsieur Bartolomé lingered a long moment
contemplating these little citadels. He noted the details of their
architecture in his notebook: the well-laid foundations, the
windows arranged along the length of the walls that rose up like
arrows, the inner courtyards, the small pools where miniature
sea creatures frisked about, all furnished with sandy material

by the admirable overseer of this creation. Monsieur Bartolomé was filled with wonder to think that such splendour could be born of so much rage and ugliness.

The tide finally rose high enough to erase all traces of these little sandcastles. As he read over his notes, Monsieur Bartolomé tried, as always, to attach some sense to the series of events he had seen unfold since the night before. He wanted to see in these things a depiction of hope itself: from storms, chaos, and upheaval resulted a structure that, although fragile and quickly carried away by the tides of the world, still left a trace in the heart – a dance, a poem.

A clearing, a bright interval.

The birds that populated the sky in these parts were not the same as those Monsieur Bartolomé had so often watched in the city, and then on the mountain. The air, then, had been traversed by dozens of coloured specks, flying like arrows escaped from a bow. Here, whiteness, the stroll of an ancient aeroplane, had taken the place of colours and speed. It's true that gulls, sterns, gannets, and other white inhabitants of the near sky did hold close commerce with saline mists, with the ocean's measured breath. Perhaps in the long run this caused the feathers to fade; perhaps this set a certain cadence.

It still happened that Monsieur Bartolomé saw these things differently. *Everything, here,* he thought, *is made for contemplation. This absence of obstacles as far as the eye can see. This silence of things that have grown so quiet as to leave nothing in space but the litany of waves and wind. These nights more vast and deep than anywhere else on earth. It seems to me that the birds, here, must be in harmony with this,* he thought. *Without ridges, points, spurs, bumps, buttes, all those aspects of landscapes to worry about, nor noises like so many contours rising up from the solid earth, they must be able to abandon themselves to their reverie with ease. And how languid are those reveries! Everything for them is slowed down. In their very structure is the seed of an observance that is at once attentive, patient, and free of the world's accelerations, completely absorbed in its delving.*

But why this whiteness of seabirds? At dusk, when he watched them moving away over the cliff, Monsieur Bartolomé murmured to himself: "The day has thrown a little of its light on their bodies. Who knows what part of the world, and above all what grieving heart, they will go to tonight, bearing comfort?"

It happened more and more often that he thought of God. This seemed to him, especially as he grew older, to be a natural movement of consciousness. After all, was not one of the roles of this same consciousness to conceive of something greater than the self? This was what nature, in its boundless inventiveness, had found to be most effective for ensuring the growth of life, its progression, or better, its continuity: the capacity for an organism to surpass, by means of creativity, its own finiteness.

But all this was not enough to make him believe or not believe, and these questions diminished in importance. It was enough for Monsieur Bartolomé to think of God, to imagine and form an image that might have lacked magic, but always remained close to human substance. Because the imagination, without a doubt, was made of this same substance: the complicated assemblies of nerves, muscles, and membranes, essential disorders of netting and curtains, conduits and winding roads, liquids and electric currents, complex industries and incredible roadworks coincided in the flesh of human beings to create this astounding workshop of forms and figures. Thus, Monsieur Bartolomé never left the strict domain from which he came: today as always, things, matter, were his most familiar terrain. In this, he was like the pebbles he trod on along the shore: in them stood the same architecture of silence, the same enclosing flesh of stars.

These thoughts that came with age and lodged themselves little by little in his mind caused him to measure the time that had passed. It had been thirty-nine years since his son disappeared. If we imagined that he was still living, a quick calculation shows that he would be fifty-one years old by now. Monsieur Bartolomé himself was now seventy-nine.

He understood this: all his life, he had devoted himself to a progressive asceticism, and bit by bit, had turned away from other beings, then from things, like so many coats separating him from a secret presence, seated in the centre of his body, in his very belly. All his life, he had been doing one thing and one thing only: walking to meet his death. The sense of this had become heightened after the child disappeared. For Monsieur Bartolomé, how, indeed, could he conceive otherwise of this disappearance without return, this unbroken silence that had settled permanently in his flesh, other than as the symbol of his own extinction come early to remind him of his human brevity? And come, also, to invite him not to die before his time, but on the contrary, to live, to live as one condemned: with the extraordinary feeling in his heart of knowing the true price of each day.

The departure of his son had also marked the beginning of a new quest, one that was unavoidable and had remained mysterious for a long time. The quest of a necessary and gradual impoverishment, an extreme simplification, in preparation for the tremendous solitude we must feel at the moment of our own end. Whether his son was alive or dead mattered little now. The important thing was that he had existed for nearly forty years in Monsieur Bartolomé's imagination – which is to say within his body. Thus his son had continuously inspired in him – and often through pain – this vast movement, this existence composed of gestures and strides, this great march to the rhythm of things, objects, stones, animals, ponds, trees, and roads – in short, of matter. Even if he had not grasped the meaning of this march very early on, Monsieur Bartolomé had still abided by it. He did not regret it: from the matter that he had so often touched, so often tread upon, so closely observed and so respected, something had always emerged – a sky or soul, one might say, that gave him affirmation on his path. Furthermore, this soul, this consciousness born of the earth – womb of all things – reminded him of his return to this same earth. The body, matter, the world in and of itself, invited him to a meeting, a tête-à-tête, a fateful moment marked with that clearest truth: the meeting with the fire that has consumed us all our lives, and in return gives to us, in the end, our true name.

He sensed a coastline within him. And more than this, he felt
that beyond this human shore lay the equivalent of marine
abysses: some sap, or blood, a whole interior sea had sculpted
pits and chasms there. When he entered the sea in front of his
house and his foot followed the curve of the slope underwater,
sooner or later there was always a moment when the rest of his
body received a sign, a message, something akin to a warning:
"Don't go any farther! Before you lies a world of gorges and
shadows!" Monsieur Bartolomé knew this world well. It was
the same one that gaped open in his belly. And he had grown
used to the echo of its warnings: something intimate told him,
over and over, to be careful – even to turn back. What? Was that
which stood so near, inside him, so very threatening, then? It
was never anything but another part of himself – and yet his
whole being seemed to rise up against this meeting. He had
felt the first hints of this vertigo before, in the hours following
the child's disappearance. Until now, he had only lived at the
edges of himself, on the fringes of his inner island. But now an
irresistible call overrode the instinct of distrust. So Monsieur
Bartolomé went forward beyond the worrisome shadows that
had always inhabited him. And from then on, he found himself
in this contradictory state that is typical of extreme depths: at
once immensely peaceful and silent, and inhabited by the presence of unknown and terrible creatures.

He thought of stories of sea monsters, hideous serpents that dragged boats and their crews down into the depths after splitting and strangling them with their long and powerful ringed bodies. He knew that such vicious monsters, greedy for flesh and turmoil, truly existed. But the sea that sheltered and fed them was different than the one whose great breath he felt beneath the boat. It was the ocean moving inside the body, that Mediterranean of our first defeats, our mediocrities and lapses, that a bad cure had undertaken to transform into terrors, phantasms, and symbolic reptiles.

One evening as he was returning from a long outing on the open sea, Monsieur Bartolomé came face to face with such an animal. The serpent, who was stretched out nearly as far as the eye could see, was calmly watching the little craft and its occupant, arrogant in their vulnerability upon the immensity of the sea. Nothing in its demeanour resembled the usual fury of sea dragons: the fearful, giant beast with bloodshot eyes stayed strangely still, resting its mild goat's gaze upon the boat. The sea, too, was peaceful. This large, smooth continent, its back turned to the newborn stars, seemed to be immersed within itself, meditating.

The enormous serpent was only a few inches away from the prow. But Monsieur Bartolomé felt no fear. He had known that a day would come when such a meeting would take place, and now, here it was. He stopped rowing. The little vessel stopped its course and bobbed gently on the wavelets.

"What do you want from me?" Monsieur Bartolomé asked the monster. But it was a question that called forth no response. Not because the answer was unsayable: the old writer knew that everything on earth has a name. It was simply a question without an answer, that's all, like objects stripped of their shadows at midday, sated by the lone, erect light.

A stretch of time passed. In the end, the boat, having drifted, ran aground on the shore. The small shock of the stem striking the sand pulled Monsieur Bartolomé from his reverie. He could no longer remember the moment he had closed his eyes.

And so Monsieur Bartolomé's soul revealed itself to be stunningly silent, though he had thought it to be as howling as the storms that came from the open sea, trailing behind them their cargo of fury. In the wake of this discovery, and even though he was convinced that all things could be definitively named, Monsieur Bartolomé felt, to a greater and greater extent, that words escaped him. This was perhaps part of his death, his own end stripping away all language, that great silencer towards which he was inexorably moving. Or perhaps this silence, as though to emphasize that it was not just a synonym for death, was also there to translate the implacable, the white, the charged absence of Monsieur Bartolomé's son. Had not this child, who had lived so briefly at his side, been permeated with silence? Did not a mystery emanate from him, a secret that his young body had only revealed parsimoniously and which could now only be related to the muteness of trees, the reticence of stones and landscapes? The body and speech seemed also to be united by a singular and fleeting reality. You would think that one called to the other, and that this call subsided until one day it stopped, the body itself sensing the arrival of its end and seeking to align with this vast and silent night that is death. Were the trees, in the sort of contemplation in which they seemed to be immersed, the subjects of such premonitions? Maybe the elm standing behind the house in the city had revealed these things to Monsieur Bartolomé's son. This would explain why the child's existence had so closely resembled a prayer.

And while he paced the beach again and again, he remembered the brief paragraph he had read one day in 2003 in "Notes from a Composition Book" by the New York writer Paul Auster: "To feel estranged from language is to lose your own body. When words fail you, you dissolve into an image of nothingness. You disappear."

One week later, Monsieur Bartolomé did disappear. The rare
and faithful walkers who came regularly to take a few steps on
the beach would not see the old man again, that solitary note
taker who seldom spoke, that collector of rocks, that tireless
census taker of earth, sky, and sea.

He had walked the whole day long, counting out the hours
and observing things. Was he not born for this and this alone:
to contemplate the procession of things, to tread upon the earth,
which is for all people both jewel case and tomb? Things: this
city, vibrant beneath its gold, this street fringed with houses,
these clouds, all these people battered by the years, their arms
full of ages gathered like fruit beneath the tree of their death,
the earth, the earth, where Monsieur Bartolomé had left so
many steps.

Then he went home. The house when he found it was
beautiful, covered in twilight. At the door, come from a far-off
forest and visibly tired from the journey, was a fox that greeted
him and whispered these words: "One day, the birds will tell
us (they who have known both earth and sky): 'Do not glorify
altitude and vertigo so. Because in truth the sky decorates itself
with stars, and in the birdsong storms rain down, and the clouds
are always there to stir up tears. Of course, the earth, with its
grasses over your bones, is no less of a liar. It is the house of your
shadows. But is it not upon the earth that the sun lays down
your shadows, and then tucks them in?' "

Later in the evening, Monsieur Bartolomé went out on the
ocean for the last time. He rowed the boat out slowly until he

reached the open sea. He took one last look at the sky ablaze with stars and then, stepping over the gunwale, slid into the black water and went under. He did not reappear.

The evening wind blew softly.

In the minutes that followed, eight whales stopped their games for a moment and emerged simultaneously from the depths of the ocean. They stayed for a long moment, observing in silence the boat that had been deserted by its master beneath the white clarity of the moon. Rising just slightly above the waves, their large backs and then their blue-and-black heads made a series of islands. Sleepless seabirds came and stood there after long crossings, like tiny airplanes come to rest their sides that had been beaten by the skies for too long.

The rowboat bounced along, and guided perhaps by habit, returned to the shore after a few hours, empty.

Empty – but not without a soul.

Days, months, and then years passed. The house, left to itself, lost its planks one by one and the wind whistled through it. The rowboat filled with sand and slowly rotted. Stars no longer flew from its hull. And so the world did its work. But Monsieur Bartolomé's soul remained, unchanged, silent, as though seated upon the old wood of the small craft. How can we tell? When the rain came, people walking on the cliff would swear that through the curtain it made in front of their eyes, they could see a tree rising up from the bottom of the rowboat. A child was there, sitting beneath the branches, watching the sea.

He took notes.

I came across *Turkana Boy* by fortuitous chance at the Bibliothèque et Archives nationales du Québec in Montreal, while searching for a book to translate as part of my master's thesis. Standing between stacks, I read this question in the third chapter: *"L'âme était donc un ciel enchevêtré à l'homme?"* ("Was the soul, then, a sky tangled in every person?") and I was captivated. I knew this was the one.

Jean-François Beauchemin's style is listing (in both the literal and the nautical sense of the word), imagistic, and punctuated with marvellous questions that are the crux of both his poetry and the central character's search for something greater than himself. I resonated deeply with all these elements. The challenge for me was to deliver the surreal images, questions, and quiet sadness of the book in a way that made the phrases in English as startling, as compelling.

I began to correspond with Jean-François early on. He was generous and encouraging, sometimes answering multiple messages about a single word – such as *"cerné,"* which means surrounded, but may also contain connotations of shadows, darkness, or even military battles. I asked what he meant by such illustrative passages as *"Il se souvenait des soirées semblable à des cales. Il y descendait comme les arbres aux racines, appuyait l'oreille à leur fer ainsi qu'on emplit un panier"* ("He remembered evenings like the hulls of ships. He descended to them like trees to their roots and pressed his ear to their iron, gathering, as though he were filling a basket") and he patiently explored them with me. But it troubled me to ask him to *explain* – because poetry shouldn't be explained, it should be lived and felt. And then a pivotal point came. It was Jean-François who pushed me (out of the nest, so to speak) to have faith in my own interpretation. He let me know that he trusted in my poetic sensibility, and urged me to take the translation firmly into my own hands. Because, of course, to be truly faithful to a work means stepping away from a too-close adherence – in terms of rhythm, words, and phrasing; it means maintaining a loyalty to the *spirit* of the work, its poetry, and delivering this into the second language with as much oddity or grace as exists in the original. Translation of poetic prose asks the translator to become a poet as well.

Since translation is always an act of furthering and response – taking a written work beyond its structural and linguistic boundaries and offering, in answer, a new text – we could also say that *movement* is integral to the work of translation: we begin in one place, or language, and end in a second one. In another sense of the word, the translator must allow herself to be moved enough to breathe new life into the work. And in the case of *Turkana Boy*, movement went one step further: the process of translating this novel inspired me to write. Many of the pieces in my book, *Everything, Now* (Brick Books, 2012), took inspiration from this work of translation and could be called a kind of resonant response. Works of literature that are moving are the most powerful ones – because they incite reciprocal movement.

This translation has taken me on several journeys: to New York City to accept a PEN American Translation Fund Award (where I had the chance to see the Turkana Boy exhibit at the American Museum of Natural History); to Rotterdam and Marfa for residencies; and finally to Toronto Island where I completed revisions of the novel to the sounds of crickets and the lake. I have lived among the words of this remarkable book for some years. It is a great pleasure to share them, now, with you.

# Translator's Acknowledgements

I would like to thank Sherry Simon and Héloïse Duhaime for their considerable help in the early stages of the translation, Benoît Chaput for afternoon reflections, and Raphaël Beaulieu for cheerful consults at the last critical moment. Thank you to everyone at Talonbooks (including former director, Karl Siegler, for first believing in the book) – Kevin Williams, Greg Gibson, Les Smith, and especially to Garry Thomas Morse, and to Ann-Marie Metten, who worked patiently and insightfully with me (word by word, comma by comma). I am grateful to the PEN American Translation Fund and the Lannan Foundation for their support. And warm thanks to Jean-François, for such gracious encouragement, and marvellous questions.

# Reproduction Permissions

**Jessica Moore** is an author and translator. Her first book, *Everything, Now*, part lyric, part memoir, is forthcoming in Fall 2012 from Brick Books. She is a former Lannan writer-in-residence and winner of a 2008 PEN American Translation Fund Award for her translation of a section from *Turkana Boy*. Her poems and translations have appeared in literary journals across Canada and the United States. She is a member of the Literary Translators' Association of Canada, where she worked while completing her master's thesis in Translation Studies. She also writes songs and plays the banjo – her band, Charms, launched a self-titled album in 2010 in Toronto.

After graduating from the University of Montreal in French Studies, **Jean-François Beauchemin** worked for ten years as a director at Radio-Canada. In 2004, he began to work full time as a writer. A prolific author, to date he has published many novels, short stories, and two collections of poetry, all warmly welcomed. These include *Le jour des corneilles*, awarded the Prix France–Québec in 2004, and *La fabrication de l'aube*, which won the Quebec booksellers' prize in 2007. Meditative of mind and attentive to the strange coexistence of body and soul, Jean-François Beauchemin offers thoughtful work, lucid and always imbued with poetry rooted in reality.